For Robyn
J. E.

For Hugo
V. C.

First U.S. edition 2005

Library of Congress Cataloging-in-Publication Data is available.

Library of Congress Catalog Card Number 2003069621

ISBN 0-7636-2554-X

4 6 8 10 9 7 5 3

Printed in China

This book was typeset in Beta Bold.
The illustrations were done in watercolor.

Candlewick Press
2067 Massachusetts Avenue
Cambridge, Massachusetts 02140

visit us at www.candlewick.com

No Place Like Home

Jonathan Emmett

illustrated by Vanessa Cabban

CANDLEWICK PRESS
CAMBRIDGE, MASSACHUSETTS

"Hot-diggety!"
said Mole as he climbed
out of the ground one morning.
It was a beautiful day. The sun was shining.
And there were flowers everywhere.

Suddenly Mole's burrow seemed
very small and dark and dull.
"Why should I live underground,"
Mole said to himself,
"when I could live
somewhere BIG
and BRIGHT
and BEAUTIFUL instead!"

So Mole
set off in search
of a new home.

He hadn't
gone far when
he came across
Hedgehog.

"Hello, Mole,"
said Hedgehog. "Where are you off to?"

"I'm looking for a new home," explained Mole.
"Somewhere
BIG and
BRIGHT and
BEAUTIFUL."

"I know just the place!"
said Hedgehog.
"Follow me!"

"So what do you think?"
asked Hedgehog
as they crawled into a hollow log.
Mole tried to feel at home
in the log, but the wind
was whistling right
through it.

"Well,"
said Mole, shivering,
"it's very BIG—but it's too drafty
for me. I'd like somewhere
a little more snug."

"What's up?"
asked Squirrel.

Mole and Hedgehog
had just crawled
out of the log
when they saw
Squirrel.

"I'm looking
for a new home,"
explained Mole.
"Somewhere
BRIGHT
and BEAUTIFUL."

"And SNUG,"
added
Hedgehog.

"I know just the place!"
said Squirrel.
"Follow me!"

"So what do you think?"
said Squirrel as Mole clambered
into an empty bird's nest.

Mole tried to feel
at home in the nest. But he was
too afraid of falling out.

"Well," he said, "it's very BRIGHT —
but it's too dangerous for me.
I'd like somewhere a
little safer."

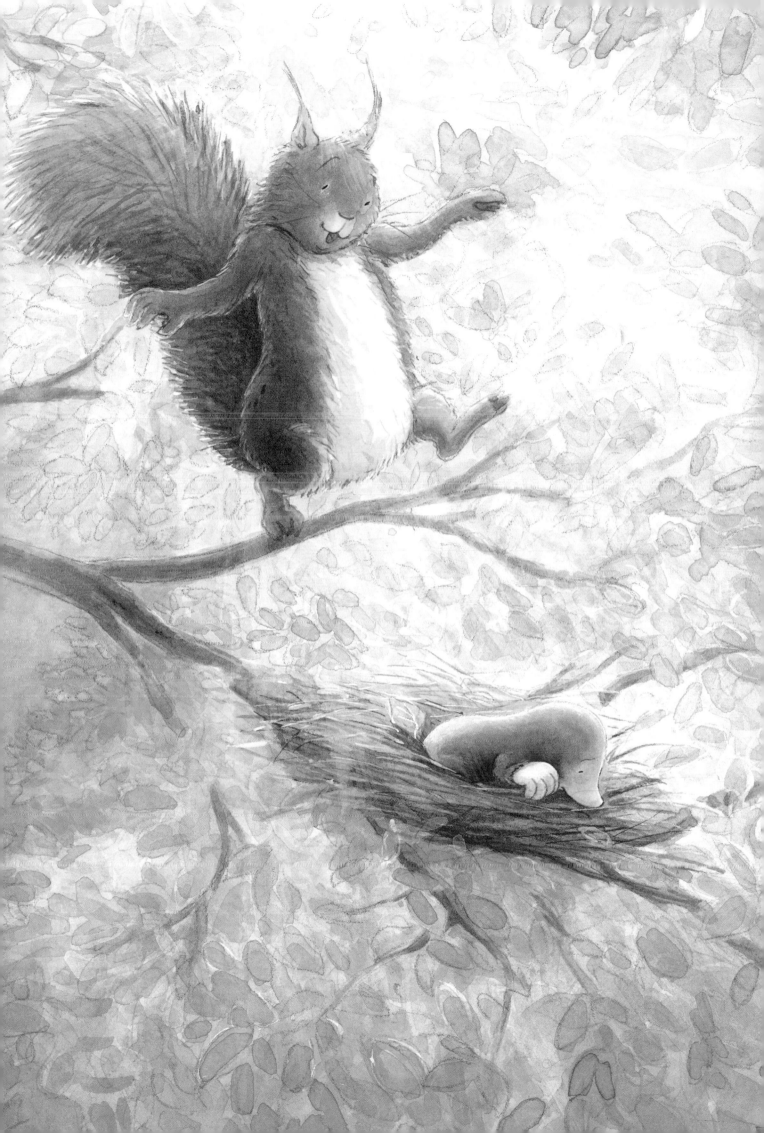

Hedgehog, Squirrel, and Mole
had just climbed down to the ground
when Rabbit came bounding up.

"What's happening?" asked Rabbit.

"I'm looking for a new home,"
explained Mole.
"Somewhere BEAUTIFUL."

"And SNUG," added Hedgehog.

"And SAFE," added Squirrel.

"I know just the place!"
said Rabbit.

Rabbit led Mole,
Squirrel, and Hedgehog
to a little stream.

"Over here!" she said,
hopping easily
from stone to stone.

"So what do you think?"
said Rabbit as they scrambled
into a hollow beside
a sparkling waterfall.

Mole tried to feel at home
in the hollow, but he kept
getting splashed.

"Well," he said, "it's very
BEAUTIFUL—
but it's too wet for me.
I'd like somewhere
a little more dry."

It was getting late, and Mole
still hadn't found his new home.

"I didn't think it would
be this difficult," sighed Mole.

"Don't worry. We'll find somewhere," said Rabbit.

"We just need to give
it some thought," said Squirrel.

So they all sat down and thought,
and thought, and thought, until . . .

"I know just the place,"
said Mole.

He led Squirrel, Hedgehog,
and Rabbit back across the woodland
to a familiar-looking hole.

"But this is your OLD home!"
said Rabbit, Hedgehog, and Squirrel.

"I know," said Mole happily.
"Isn't it WONDERFUL?
It's not BIG or BRIGHT or BEAUTIFUL.
But it feels
just right to me."

It was dark outside, and a storm
was sweeping across the woodland.
But everyone was very
comfortable down
in Mole's burrow.

"It's so SNUG,"
said Hedgehog.

"And SAFE,"
said Squirrel.

"And DRY,"
said Rabbit.

"Yes," said Mole
contentedly.
"There's no place
like home!"